Something on the Hill

written by
Jane Kohuth

illustrated by
Sonia Sánchez

a·s·b
anne schwartz books

One morning Field Mouse woke up in her nest.
 She had been sleeping through the cold and ice and snow.
But something had changed. Something was out there,
calling to her. Something on the Hill.

As she scrambled through the
underbrush, Field Mouse spotted
Gray Squirrel taking out his last acorns.
"Hi, hi, Mousie!" he chattered.
"Squirrel," said Field Mouse, "Something
is on the Hill! I can hear it."

"Yes, yes, the Hill! I can smell it!" chattered Squirrel.
"Come with me," said Field Mouse. "Help me find the Something."
"Sure, sure!" Gray Squirrel skittered to the ground.

When a shadow passed over the two friends, they froze, trying to be invisible. But it was only Doe, stepping silently through the woods.

"Hello," said Doe. "And where are you hurrying today?"

"We're going to the Hill," said Field Mouse. "To see what's there."

"I, too, am going to the Hill," said Doe. "I will go with you."

When the little group came to a wide stream,
they saw that the ice had melted.

The water rushed over the rocks.
On the far bank, a turtle sat on a fallen log.
"Heading to the Hill," he observed.
"You know about the Hill, too?" asked Field Mouse.
"Oh, yes," said Turtle. "It goes like this each year.
And I have been in these woods many years."
"Come with us!" called Gray Squirrel.
"I suppose I might as well," said Turtle.

Doe waded through the stream. Gray Squirrel leapt from rock to rock. But the water was racing and tumbling, and Field Mouse did not know how she would get to the other side. Frightened, she cried out to her friends.

"I will help," said Turtle.

Turtle plopped into the water and slowly swam across.
"Climb onto my back, Little One," he said.
Field Mouse scrabbled onto Turtle's slippery shell
and held on tightly.

At last they clambered up the bank.

Gallump bump. Gallump bump. Turtle lumbered along behind the others. Field Mouse slowed her paws to keep her new friend company.

The group followed the stream to
a pond, where ice still lay in the middle,
like a cracked dinner plate.
    The Mallard Ducks He, She, and They
perched on it, turning their beaks to the
sun. They saw the animals trooping past.
    "Something is afoot," said He.
    "Something on the Hill," agreed She.
    And they waddled out to join the band.

At the entrance to a cave, the animals paused.
"We should wake the Bears," Field Mouse whispered.
But everyone was afraid of the Bears.
"The Something is important," said Doe.
"The Bears shouldn't miss it."

So Field Mouse held her ears tall
and marched into the cave.
"Wake up, Bears! Something is waiting
for us on the Hill!" she squeaked bravely.

Mother Bear opened one eye, and the
two Bear Cubs yawned. The Bears stared at
Field Mouse. She thought they looked hungry.

"Come, children," said Mother Bear finally in her deep, rumbling voice. "Time to wake up and follow the little mouse."

Field Mouse's whiskers relaxed, and together they stepped out of the cave.

When the parade emerged from the trees,
there stood the Hill, awash in sunlight.

Up and up, higher and higher, the animals climbed.

Something old like a turtle,
and new like a duckling.

Something just as gentle and
just as important as a mouse.

At the tippy-top, Field Mouse looked down at her tired paws.

And then she saw it!

It was the Something!

Something sprightly like a squirrel,
and quiet like a deer.

Something blinking in the sun,
like a bear waking after a long sleep.

"It's here!" cried Field Mouse, and her friends rushed to see it poking from the earth: a leafy shoot, tiny and green.

Spring had come!